Moo Pie

IN THE

MOONLIGHT

Story by **Beth Olmo**   Illustrated by **Erin Blunt**

Peach Juice Publishing

For my husband, Orlando. Without your unshakeable faith and abiding love for me, this would have been impossible. 愛してるよ! -Beth

For Emalyn, my little Pumpkin Pie, whose reliable naps and independent nature enabled me to create work that makes her daddy proud. -Erin

Moo Pie in the Moonlight
Text copyright © 2010 by Beth Olmo
Illustration copyright © 2010 by Erin Blunt

Book Design by Erin Blunt
The text for this book is set in Typo3.

Peach Juice Publishing
Orders: www.PJPublishing.com

ISBN: 978-0-578-06991-3
First Edition

CPSIA Compliance Information: Batch #1110.
For further information contact
RJ Communications, NY, NY, 1-800-621-2556

The Story of Moo Pie

Moo Pie was a very handsome tuxedo cat who lived on a mountain a long time ago. When he was born I thought he looked like a little black and white cow, so I named him Moo. He was such a sweet boy, always relaxed, and he loved to take naps in funny places.

I came into the kitchen one day to find him asleep in the sink. I took him out, but he jumped back in. We did this a couple of times before I gave up and turned on the water just a bit. Most other cats would have run away when the water touched them, but Moo just looked up and meowed quietly. I had to wait until he was good and ready to get out of the sink. So for a while I called him Moo-Wash.

Not long after, I found him sleeping in a clean pie dish on the table! He was curled up tight so he could fit, and fast asleep with his tail across his nose. He was sleeping so deeply and looked so peaceful that I didn't have the heart to wake him. From then on, he was Moo Pie.

Moo always loved strolling through the grass in the evening, watching fireflies, and sleeping on the windowsill in the moonlight. He knew just how a summer evening should be enjoyed.

The long summer day is finally done...

...and dark time chases away the sun.

Crickets sing songs, fireflies take flight...

...and Moo Pie dances

in the moonlight.

Hooting things hoot, creeping things creep...

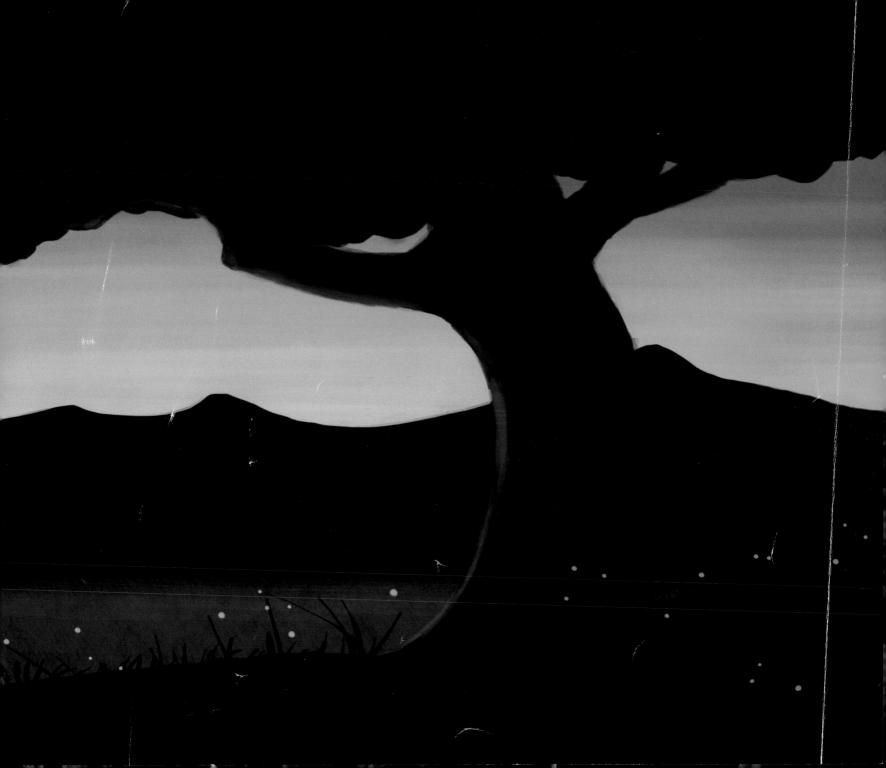

...and all the mountain settles down to sleep.

The wind whispers low as the moon climbs high...

...and Moo Pie strolls

in the moonlight.

The dark gets quiet,

and the quiet gets dark.

Bo doesn't whinny, and Buster doesn't bark.

Stars shine silent

in the velvet sky...

...and Moo Pie bathes

in the moonlight.

Today is long gone,

tomorrow yet to come...

...too late for bees to buzz,

or hummingbirds to hum.

Little ones snuggle close

to their mothers' sides...

...and Moo Pie dreams in the moonlight.

Beth Olmo is a writer, entrepreneur, and proud Navy wife with a widely varied background. She has enjoyed working in radio and television, teaching English to preschoolers and adults in Japan, and contributing articles to OkinawaHai.com. Beth has been a life-long animal lover, and never fails to be entertained and inspired by her pets' antics. When she's not planning their future world travels, Beth can be found playing in the waters off Okinawa, Japan with her husband Orlando and their dog, Sky.

Erin Blunt brings a great deal of talent and skill to every project. She holds a B.A. in Illustration from the Savannah College of Art and Design and enjoys working digitally. Erin has a passion for portraits, and was also the Book Designer for "Takako and the Great Typhoon" (Kelly Garcia, 2009). One of Erin's long-term goals is to be well known for her children's book illustrations. When not hard at work, Erin enjoys life in beautiful Okinawa, Japan with her husband Drew, sweet baby daughter Emalyn, and their canine family member, Copernicus.